Bromley Climbs Uluru

Alan & Patricia Campbell

LANSDOWNE

Here is Bromley Bear. It is early morning in the red Australian desert, and Bromley is collecting firewood. He is about to boil the billy for a cup of tea.

Bromley is waiting for his friend Koala. Together they are going on a big adventure, to climb Uluru, the most splendid rock in the whole world. Uluru is like a great mountain in the middle of Australia, and Bromley and his friend must travel a long way to find it.

But where is Koala?

Here is Koala. He and Bromley drink their tea, then they go exploring.

'Just look at this big mud pie,' Koala says.

'That's not a mud pie,' Bromley says. 'That's a termite mound. Termites are like ants. They build these mounds really high to keep themselves cool on hot days. Come on, Koala, we have a long way to go.'

'Still looks like a mud pie to me,' Koala mutters as he climbs down the tree.

There are camels in the outback of Australia. Here are some, waiting for Bromley and Koala. The friends will travel part of the way by camel.

Bromley chooses a camel. His name is Cranky Clive — and he is bad-tempered, stubborn and just plain cantankerous.

Bromley yells, 'Go, Camel, go!'

Cranky Clive snorts, spits, stamps his feet, then suddenly he takes off.

Poor Bromley holds on fast. 'This camel is crazy!' he yells.

Cranky Clive soon stops, and Bromley falls off, right into
a prickly bush.

'Oh dear,' he says, pulling out the prickles. 'My camel has run away.
And where is Koala?'

'Here I am,' Koala says. 'Lucky for us I held onto the camel's tail!
Where do we go now?'

'Let's climb to the top of that big cliff to find our way,'
Bromley says.

So up they go, and they sit on the rock, to look out over the hot land.

'I see a dry lake over there,' says Bromley. 'Let's go down and
have a look.'

Bromley climbs down the cliff. On the edge of the dry lake, he sees a baobab tree.

He walks onto the bed of the lake and there he meets a snake.

'Hey, Snake. Where are you going? It's hot here on the mud. You could shrivel up.'

'I'm on my way to visit a friend,' Snake says, 'but I'm so thirsty. Can you give me some water?'

'I'm afraid my water bottle is empty,' Bromley says. 'But you stay here, and I will find us some water.' Then clever Bromley goes to the baobab tree, because he knows that baobab trees store water in their trunks all through the dry season.

Bromley makes a little hole near the bottom of the baobab tree. Then he takes a tiny tap from his secret pocket, puts it in the hole and turns it.

Here comes the water, dripping into Bromley's water bottle. When the bottle is full, he takes out the tap and plugs the hole with a twig.

Bromley gives the snake a drink. 'Here, drink the water slowly.'

'You saved my life. Thank you,' hisses the snake. Then he slithers away to find a shady place to rest.

Bromley hears Koala calling from the bush. 'Cooee! Cooee!'

'I'm coming, Koala,' Bromley calls.

Bromley cannot see Koala, but he follows the sound of his voice.
It comes from inside a very fat baobab tree.

'That is the biggest baobab tree I have ever seen,' Bromley says to himself. 'I wonder if bunyips live in it, or goblins, or perhaps a witch, or a giant lizard?'

But Koala is here somewhere, so in Bromley must go.

He climbs into a dark hole in the tree. Inside, he feels coolness on his fur. This is just the place to be on a hot day. But it is spooky too.

'Koala, where are you?' he calls.

Then he looks up through the hole and sees light above.
He starts to climb towards it, right up the middle of the baobab tree.

Just as Bromley reaches the top, someone says, 'Boo!'

It is Bromley's friend, Skye, the flying unicorn. She has flown to the top of the tree to meet Bromley and Koala.

'Oh!' Bromley says, 'what a fright you gave me. Where is Koala?'

'He's climbing down the tree. We have a journey to make,' Skye says. 'Have you forgotten we are all going to Uluru?'

'Of course not,' Bromley says, then oops! He loses his footing and falls back into the dark hole. Thump, bump, crash. 'Ouch!' Bromley grumbles.

At the bottom, Koala and Skye have a good laugh and brush the dust off Bromley. Then the friends set off together through the desert.

Skye the magic unicorn takes her friends to a billabong, where there are beautiful coloured rocks.

'This is a strange place,' Koala says, sitting in a small tree.

Bromley puts on his Aussie sunhat. 'This is the Valley of Magic Rainbows. When the last drops of rain fall from a shower, coloured lights flow from these rocks and go right across the sky, especially for children to see.'

Skye says, 'There's a pot of gold at the end of every rainbow.'

'No there isn't,' Koala says. 'I once followed a rainbow to the end and all I found was a soggy bog. And I fell in, too.'

'These rocks are magic, just the same,' Bromley says. 'Let's stay here for the night.'

The friends set off early the next day, but soon the sand is very hot. They still have a long way to go to reach Uluru, the biggest rock in the world.

Then they come to a plain that is just full of rocks. 'What a spooky place,' Skye says.

Bromley explains. 'A long time ago this was a forest, and the tall stumps were trees. Then the wind came along and blew sand over them. Under the sand, the trees turned into rock. Now the sand has blown away again, and these rocks are still here.'

'Shall we climb one, Bromley?' Koala says.

'What a good idea. Then we can see the way to Uluru,' Bromley agrees.

Sure enough, Bromley can see the way to Uluru from the top of a pinnacle. 'There is our path! Not far to go now!'

Bromley leads his friends across the hot red sand, and stops by a bush. He looks at the biggest rock in the world, and gasps. 'Wow, isn't it huge! I can't wait to climb Uluru.'

'It's too big for me,' Koala says. 'I'll wait for you here, Bromley.'

'So will I,' Skye says, nibbling some green leaves. 'We'll meet you at the bottom in the shade.'

'All right,' Bromley says bravely. 'Here I go.' And off he walks alone towards Uluru.

The closer Bromley gets to Uluru, the bigger it looks.
When Bromley gets to the base, he cannot even see the top.

With a mighty heave, he throws his rope up the rock until it catches.
Then he pulls his plump little body up the rope, using all his strength.

The rock face is slippery and dangerous, but still Bromley climbs, not daring to look down.

He feels himself falling, slipping on the rock, but the rope holds.
Thank goodness, Bromley is safe.

He starts to climb again.

Bromley's heart is thumping in his chest. He pulls himself up and up. At last, he is on top of Uluru.

'Hurray!' Bromley says. The sound of his own voice makes him feel brave.

He unties the rope and walks off to explore the most splendid rock in the world.

What will he find? He would like to discover something big, like a dinosaur bone.

Then he sees something moving on the top of the rock.
What is it? Bromley goes closer.

Suddenly Bromley is face to face with a dingo. He stands very still, and in a small bear voice he says, 'Hello, my name's Bromley. What's yours?'

The dingo says, 'I am Kurpanga, a keeper of this rock. You look tired and thirsty, Bromley. Come with me.'

Bromley and Kurpanga sit by a pool. Bromley drinks the cool, clear water, and tells Kurpanga about his dangerous climb.

Kurpanga tells Bromley a safe way to climb down again. Bromley falls asleep with the dingo by his side.

When he wakes, Kurpanga the dingo is gone.

Before he leaves Uluru, Bromley makes a pile of stones. 'This will show the way to the rock pool, for other climbers,' he says.

He is so happy: he has travelled to the middle of Australia, and climbed Uluru, the biggest rock in the world.

Then Bromley goes carefully down, the way the dingo told him.

In the bushes at the bottom are Skye and Koala. 'We were worried about you,' Koala says. Skye gives Bromley a little kiss on the end of his nose.

'Hm,' Bromley grunts. 'Let's go. We have more things to do, more things to see.'

So the three friends say goodbye to Uluru, and get ready for another Aussie adventure.

Published by Lansdowne Publishing Pty Limited
Level 5, 70 George Street NSW 2000, Australia

Managing Director: Jane Curry
Production Manager: Sally Stokes
Publishing Manager: Cheryl Hingley

First published 1993

© Copyright: Alan & Patricia Campbell 1993
© Copyright design: Lansdowne Publishing Pty Limited 1993

Designed by Kathie Baxter Smith on Quark Express
Set in 14 pt Times
Printed in Singapore by Tien Wah Press (Pte) Ltd

National Library of Australia Cataloguing-in-Publication data

Campbell, Alan.
Bromley Climbs Uluru.

ISBN 1 86302 323 2.

1. Bears - Juvenile fiction. I. Campbell Patricia (Patricia Anne Pemberthy). II. Title

A823.3

All rights reserved. Subject to the Copyright Act 1968, no part of this publication may be reproduced, stored in a retrieval system, or transmitted, in any form, or by any means, electronic, mechanical, photocopying, recording, or otherwise, without the prior written permission of the publisher.

The authors and publisher wish to assure readers that none of the photographs in this book taken at or purporting to be of Uluru were shot in protected sites, and the sacredness of the land has been fully respected.